Math Tricks

WRITTEN BY KATHY SCHULZ & ILLUSTRATED BY ANN CARANCI

CONTENTS

Pioneer Valley Educational Press, Inc.

"Eat your berries, Tidbit,"
said Mrs. Scurry.

"But I don't like berries," said Tidbit.

"I'm sorry you don't like them,
but berries are good for chipmunks,
so you must take at least ten bites,"
replied Mrs. Scurry.

3

"Ten bites? That's too many!"
said Tidbit.

"Well, can you take one bite?"
asked Mrs. Scurry.

"Yes, that's easy. I can do that,"
said Tidbit. He took one bite.

"Can you take two bites?"
asked Mrs. Scurry.

"Yes, that's easy. I can do that, too,"
said Tidbit. He took two more bites.

4

"Can you take three bites?"
asked Mrs. Scurry.

"Yes, that's easy. I can do that,"
said Tidbit. He took three more bites.

"Can you take four bites?"
asked Mrs. Scurry.

"Yes, that's easy. I can do that, too,"
said Tidbit. He took four more bites.

chomp
chomp
chomp
chomp
chomp
chomp
chomp
chomp
5

"Can you take ten bites?"
asked Mrs. Scurry.

"No, that's way too hard!" said Tidbit.

"No, it's not," laughed Mrs. Scurry.
"You have already taken ten bites,
and now you're done!"

Tidbit sometimes forgot how clever
his mother was about numbers.

"How did you do that?" asked Tidbit.

After his mother showed him
how she had tricked him
into taking ten bites,
Tidbit came up with a plan
to trick his brother, Morsel.

7

CHAPTER TWO Tidbit Tricks Morsel

Tidbit didn't like looking for food
for the winter, but his brother
was very good at finding acorns.
Morsel had already found
a lot of acorns.

When Morsel got home, Tidbit asked,
"May I have twenty of your acorns?"

"No way!" said Morsel.
"I have been working
for months to collect acorns
so I'll have something
to eat in the winter.
Twenty acorns is a lot!"

"Well, will you give me two acorns?" asked Tidbit.

"Sure," said Morsel. "It's not too hard to find that many." He gave Tidbit two acorns.

"Will you give me four acorns?" asked Tidbit.

"Sure," said Morsel. "It's not too hard to find that many." He gave Tidbit four more acorns.

"Will you give me six acorns?"
asked Tidbit.

"Sure," said Morsel. "It's not too hard
to find that many." He gave Tidbit
six more acorns.

"Will you give me eight acorns?"
asked Tidbit.

"Okay, but that's it," said Morsel.
He gave Tidbit eight more acorns.

"Will you give me twenty acorns?"
asked Tidbit.

"No, that's too many!" said Morsel.

"No, it's not," said Tidbit.
"You just gave me twenty acorns.
Thanks!"

"You've been doing math with Mom
again, haven't you?" asked Morsel.

"Yup!" said Tidbit.

"OK, how did you do that?"
asked Morsel.

Tidbit showed Morsel
how he had tricked him
into giving up twenty acorns.
Then they came up with a plan
to trick their dad.

CHAPTER THREE Dad Gets Tricked

"How many seeds do we want?" asked Tidbit.

"Let's get thirty," said Morsel.

"Whoa! That's a lot of seeds," said Tidbit. "This is going to be hard."

"Come on," said Morsel. "We can do it."

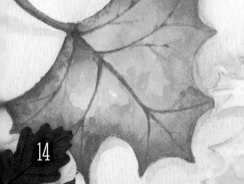

"Hey, Dad?" asked Tidbit.
"Will you give us thirty
of your seeds?"

"Well, I will share,
but I think thirty
is too many," said Mr. Scurry.

"Will you give us
six seeds?" asked Tidbit.

"Sure, six isn't too many,"
said Mr. Scurry.
He handed over six seeds.

"Will you give us seven seeds?"
asked Morsel.

"Sure, seven isn't too many,"
said Mr. Scurry. He handed over
seven more seeds.

"Will you give us eight seeds?"
asked Tidbit.

"Sure, eight isn't too many,"
said Mr. Scurry. He handed over
eight more seeds.

"Will you give us nine seeds?"
asked Morsel.

"Sure, but that's it!" said Mr. Scurry.
He handed over nine more seeds.

"Will you give us thirty seeds?"
asked Tidbit.

"No, that is way too many!"
said Mr. Scurry.

"No, it's not," said Tidbit. "You just gave
us thirty seeds. Thanks!"

"Morsel, have you been doing math
with Tidbit again?" asked Mr. Scurry.

"Yes, sir," said Morsel.

"Well, good for you," said Mr. Scurry.
"Just make sure that you each get
an even number of seeds."

"OK, Dad," laughed Tidbit.
"Hey, Morsel, will you give me
twenty seeds?"

"Oh no, here we go again," said Morsel.
"Didn't I just give you twenty acorns?"